Wayfarer's Moon ®

Thanks!

[signature] 11
ECC

Wayfarer's Moon

Wayfarer's Moon: Volume 1: The Road From Southfield is published by:
Creator's Edge Press
206 South Meridian Puyallup WA 98371

Published and distributed exclusively by Creator's Edge Press. Creator's Edge Press and its logos are tm and c 2010 by Creator's Edge Press.

Wayfarer's Moon and Single Edge Studios Inc are registered trademarks of Single Edge Studios Inc.
All materials are © 2008-2010 Single Edge Studios Inc. All rights reserved. No part of this book may be reproduced in any form (including electronic) without permission in writing from Single Edge Studios Inc except for brief passages in connection with a review. This is a work of fiction and any resemblance herein to actual persons, events or institutions is purely coincidental.

Story by Jason Janicki and Leigh Kellogg. Written by Jason Janicki.
Pencils and Inks by Leigh Kellogg. Colors by Leigh Kellogg, Leah Rivera, and Lamplighter Studios, Inc.
Lettering by Jason Janicki. Cover pencils by Leigh Kellogg. Cover painted by Lee Moyer.
Logos by Leigh Kellogg. Fonts by Blambot www.blambot.com.

These materials originally appeared from April 2008 through September 2009 at www.wayfarersmoon.com and were collected in Wayfarer's Moon Issues #1-6.

Write Wayfarer's Moon: mail@wayfarersmoon.com

First Edition: February 2011. PRINTED IN CANADA
ISBN: 978-098279341-1

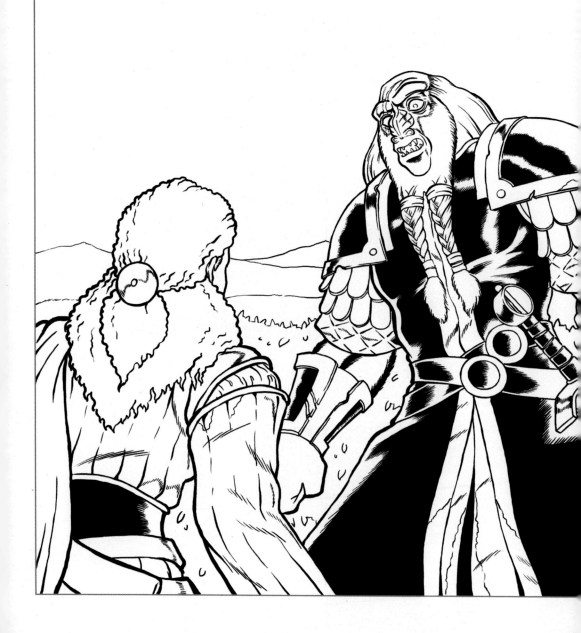

**Story by Jason Janicki
and Leigh Kellogg**

**Written and Lettered by
Jason Janicki**

**Penciled and Inked by
Leigh Kellogg**

**Colored by
Leigh Kellogg, Leah Rivera,
and Lamplighter Studios, Inc.**

**Cover Penciled by Leigh Kellogg
Cover Painted by Lee Moyer**

By Jason and Leigh
www.wayfarersmoon.com

Jason:
For my dad,
'cause he believed I could

Leigh:
For my mother,
who taught me to draw

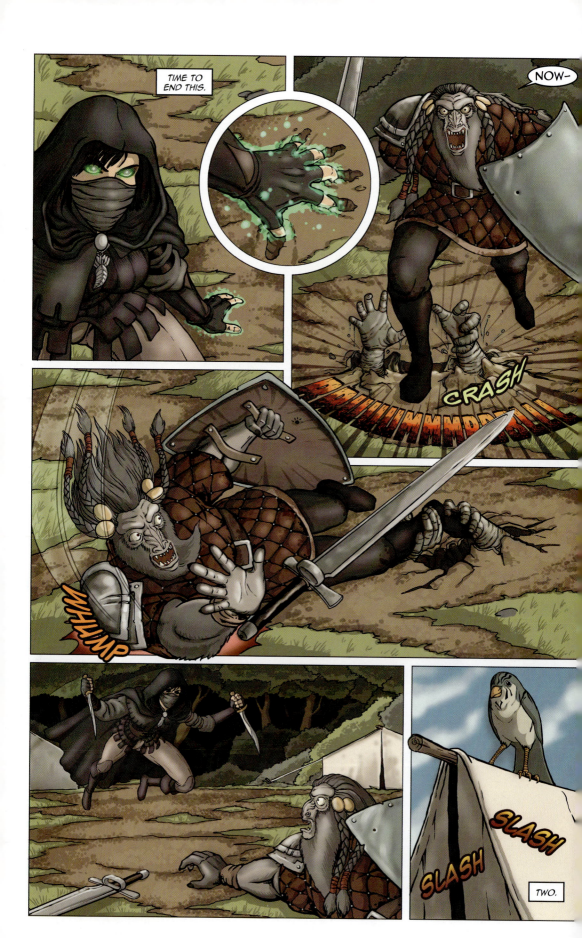

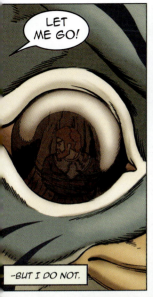

THERE CAN BE NO HESITATION, NO MISTAKES.

I SWEAR BY EARTH AND SKY I WILL BE FREE.

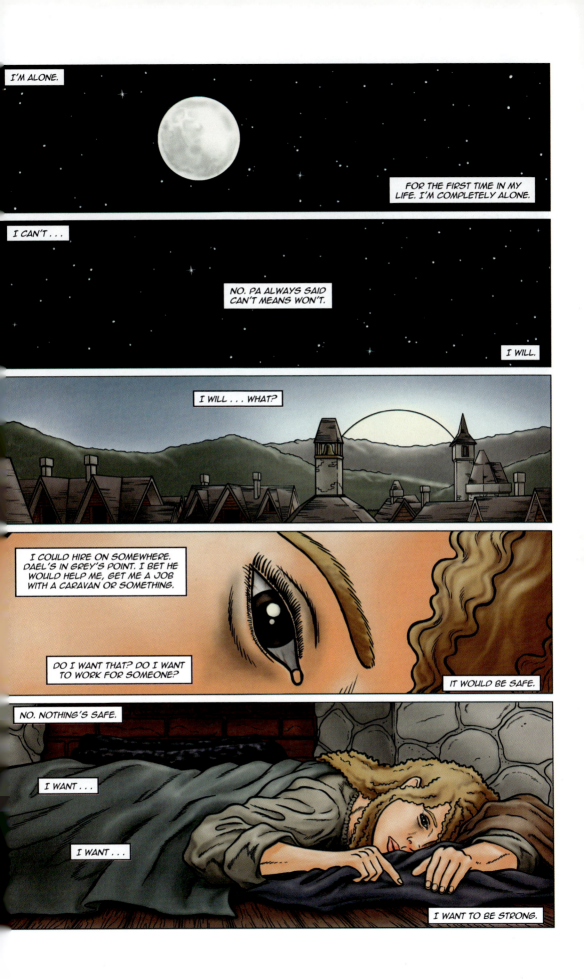

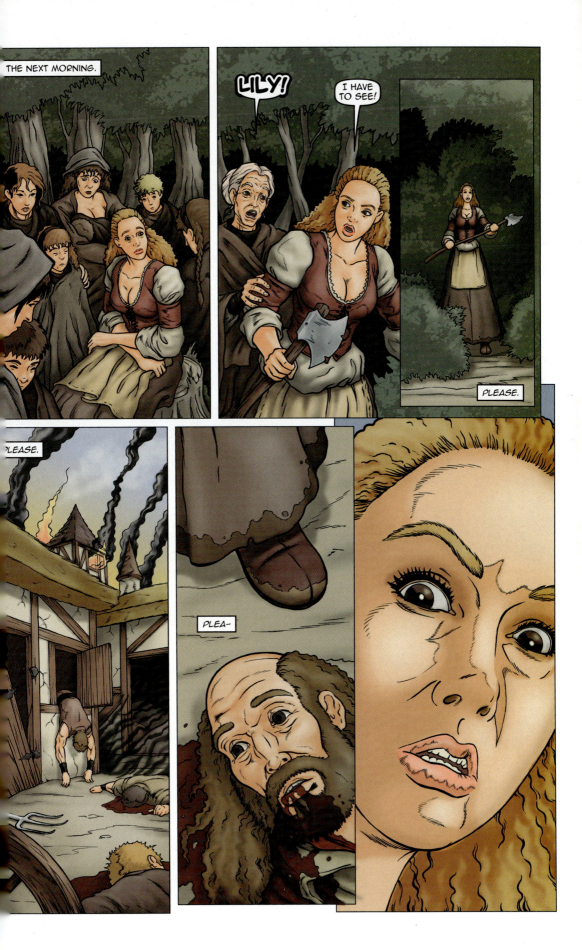

chapter 4: shadow of arken

BREMIS, THREE DAYS LATER.

THEIR SCENT LEADS HERE, BUT THERE'S TOO MANY PEOPLE, IT WILL TAKE TOO LONG TO FIND.

THESE HUMANS ARE NOT USED TO MY KIND, BEST NOT TO ATTRACT TOO MUCH ATTENTION.

THERE.

EXCUSE ME.

GASP!

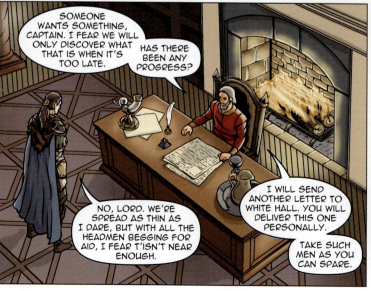

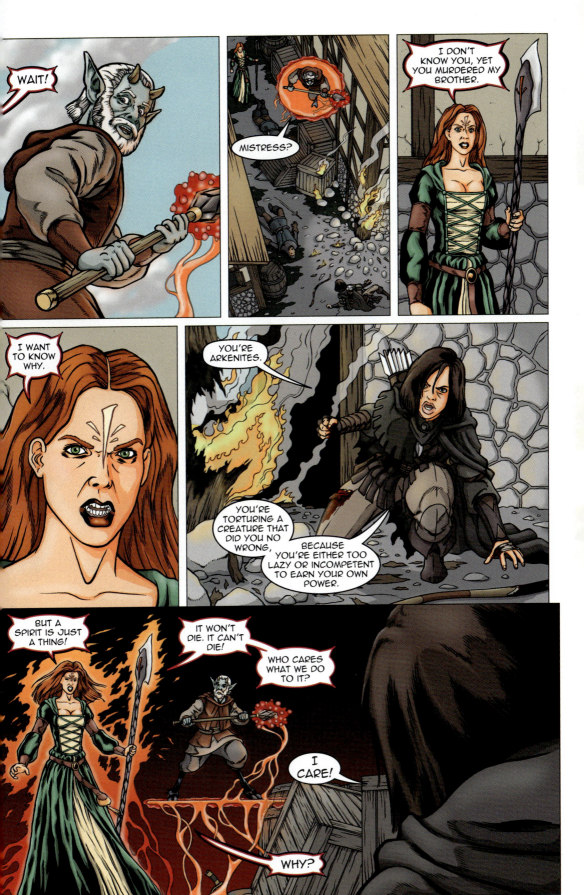

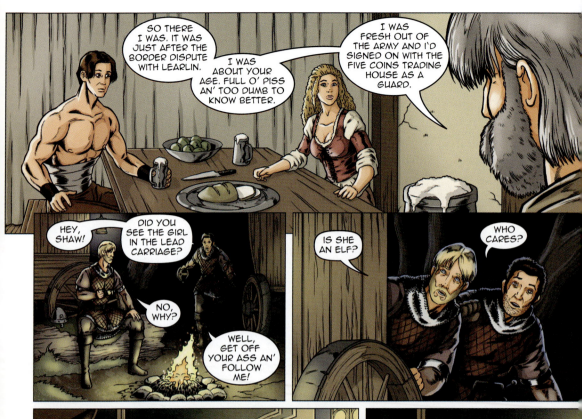

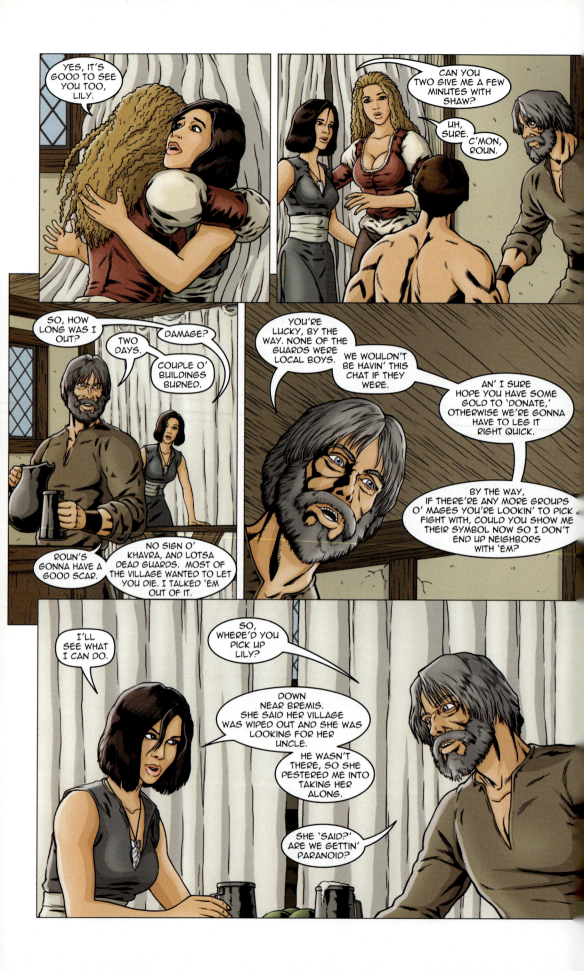

tales from the fireside:
the scale war

The old man took a long drink from his mug of ale as the children settled in front of him. He waited for them to quiet down, pointedly staring at one boy who kept talking until the other children shushed him. "Now then," he said. "What do you want to hear?"

A little girl's hand shot up. "Akara and the wolf!"

"No, Elli. I told that one just last week."

"Llevan at the Gates!" a boy almost shouted.

"The one 'bout Donnaryn's Forge" another boy said, waving his hand.

"How about a history, Grandad?" a woman said from her seat at a loom.

"A history," the old man muttered. He looked past the children, at the rough hewn log walls of the hall, his hand going to scratch at his white beard. He nodded. "I'll tell the oldest history I know, 'bout the greatest war ever fought. The Scale War."

The children looked at one another and even the adults paused in their tasks.

"I don't recall ever hearin' that one, grandfather," a young man said from beside the fire, where he was mending rope.

"That's 'cause I don't tell it much!"

There were a few chuckles, and then the old man took another pull of ale.

"A long, long time ago," he began. "There was a great war. The biggest, bloodiest war ever known."

"Did you fight in the war, Grandad?" asked Elli.

The old man smiled. "I ain't that old. This happened even before my grandfather's grandfather was born."

"Was this before the Empire fell?" asked a boy.

"Yes, even before that."

"Children! Let grandfather continue" said another woman.

"As I said," continued the old man. "This was the greatest war ever known. It started far to the west, when a great army of lizard folk called the S'karch crossed the Scale Pass an' attacked the Elven villages on the Black Water Lake."

"The Elves weren't expectin' nothin' an' had no chance. They got slaughtered even before they knew they were in a battle. The Elf King heard 'bout it though and soon the Elven army marched to meet the lizards and a big battle was fought. Now, there was a lot a' S'Karch an' it's said any one of 'em was tougher than any three M'Kott you'd care to pick. It took a lot to kill just one of the lizards an' though the Elves fought hard, they couldn't stop 'em. The S'karch woulda rolled right over the Elves if they hadn't run for the lake."

"In just a few months, the S'karch took the entire western side of the lake an' started to cross. The Elves set up on the opposite bank an' shot the hell outta them as they came outta over the water. The lizards were held up for a while, but eventually they got across and headed into the woods."

"Now, everybody knows you don't fight an Elf in the woods, but- "

"Why not?" asked Elli.

"Why not what?"

"Why don't you fight Elves in the woods?"

"'cause that's where they're born. They know the woods so well, a whole army of 'em could march by ten feet away an' you'd never notice. Anyway, where was I?"

"Fightin' elves in the woods," a teenage boy said.

"Right. Now, the S'Karch went right on into the woods an' found out the hard way. Eventually, they just started cuttin' the trees down rather than get shot tryin' to go through 'em."

"About this time, the lizards figured they'd go north, around the woods an' head out into the plains. An' that's when they first met Men. They had an easy time of it at first, but once the Emperor caught wind, he sent his son, Haern to take care a' them."

"Haern the Brave?" a child asked.

"That would be him. Haern took a hundred score cavalry into the plains an' kicked the cr- behinds o' the lizards right quick. The Elves heard 'bout this and sent messengers, askin' for more help. The Emperor, in his wisdom, knew that if the Elves fell, the whole S'Karch army'd be at his door an' so he sent his army an' his son to help."

"The Elves were exhausted at this point an' they were overjoyed to see Haern an' his boys. With the Men in the lead, the new allies took the fight to the lizards and pushed 'em outta the woods and back to the river. But even as they were celebratin', a new, bigger army a' S'Karch appeared an' you can guess what happened."

"They call it the Long Day. The Men and Elves locked their shields and dug in. They knew that if the lizards got past 'em, the Elven peoples'd be wiped out. They fought for a day and a night and another full day. They say the bodies were stacked so high, you could walk on 'em and look down at the tops o' the trees."

"Haern fought beside his men and refused to leave the lines, an' that's why they called him Hearn the Brave," said the old man, with a look at the children. "He killed three-score enemy captains an' broke fifty spears that day and his commanders had to carry him off the field when he finally collapsed from his wounds."

"Now, they'd managed to stop the lizards, but the allies were in no shape for another fight. An' that's when the Emperor himself appeared.

He brought an even bigger army and more than that, he'd convinced the secret people a' Illyr and the Dwarves to help! "

"What's a Dwarf?" a boy said.

"Stories say they're small, like the Kegg, but made of stone. Very strong."

"Where do they live?"

"I don't know. I don't think they exist anymore."

"What about the Kegg an' the M'Kott?" asked another boy. "Why didn't they fight?"

"I don't know. I don't think they lived here yet."

The old man paused for a drink. "Now then, united under the banner a' the Emperor, the people a' the east went after the lizards. The armies met at a place they call Red Sand an' it was the biggest battle since the gods destroyed the Blue Throne! The Dwarves held the line and crushed the lizards with their great hammers, like you or me might step on a bug. The Elves stood behind them an' filled the sky with arrows, an' no S'Karch dared lower their shield 'cause a dozen arrows'd instantly strike 'em. The Illyrian sorcerers called down lightnin' an' fire and with every wave a' their hands, two score lizards died. An' around them all rode Hearn and his cavalry, chargin' again an' again into the flanks o' the enemy, skewerin' an' tramplin S'Karch by the hundreds!"

"The S'Karch couldn't take it an' their whole army fled. The Eastern Army followed 'em and caught up with 'em at a place called the Killin' Ground. There they slaughtered the lizards without mercy. Haern himself killed their king and then the army broke their temples and destroyed everything they could find, just to teach 'em a lesson."

"An' then the army went back to the Elven woods an' to the capitol a' Baylia, the City of Brass." The old man paused. "A beautiful place," he said. "I saw it once, many years ago. He smiled. "Bought a silk scarf for 'Kara. It was green, matched her eyes."

He sat there, staring off into the distance, smiling.

"Dad?" said an older man.

"What? Oh. Where was I?" he said.

"They were having a party," said Elli promptly.

"Right. They all gathered in Baylia, the city of the Elves. They drank an' feasted an' medals were handed out an' treaties were signed an' everybody made nice. Eventually, everyone went home and Haern took the throne of Khorim after his father passed. And that's what I know, told to me by my grandfather, just like I'm tellin' you."

"But, if the Emperor was so great, why'd the Empire fall?" Elli asked.

"Another time," a woman said. "Off to bed with you. Grandpa will tell you another story tomorrow."

"Yes," said the old man. "Bed time for me too. There's work waitin' in the mornin'."

However, he continued to sit there as the other adults put away their tools, idly turning his empty mug in his hands. He was smiling.

"Dad?" said a man, who had dark green eyes, as he laid his hand on the old man's shoulder.

"There were statues in the square. Brass. When the sun hit them . . ." He glanced up.
"It was a long time ago."

"Let's go to bed, Dad."

The younger man helped his father to his feet and together they put out the last lantern, letting the door close behind them.

And the hall was quiet.

THE ELVES

The Elves
Physical Description:
Elves are typically tall and slim, with 6 feet being an average height for both males and females. A few individuals may be as tall as 6'5", but that is rare.

Elves are generally slim and are not particularly strong, with an average male being weaker than an average human male. However, they are extremely quick and dexterous and are capable of feats of dexterity and agility well beyond anything most any human could perform.

Elves are not typically any more intelligent than humans, though their long life spans (approx. 200 years) gives them a breadth of experience and knowledge that makes them seem much smarter than a typical human.

History:
The Elves are one of the oldest inhabitants of Lachryn and have lived in their forests for many thousands of years. It is said that at one time, they ruled Lachryn, though there is scant evidence of this. With their long history, the Elves have fought many wars and have had no fewer than 5 civil wars.

Culture:
The Elves are a monarchy, with a number of noble families that continually vie for power and influence. They tend to avoid violence, preferring to use legal machinations and complex plots to achieve their goals.

Most Elves live in the forest, in small communities and villages, where they farm and tend their orchards. These small hamlets provide the food for the handful of cities and the large capitol, Baylia. Most communities are self-sufficient and there is a great deal of trade between them. Surpluses are bought by either the government or the various trading houses, which then trade with the humans for grains and other commodities.

The Elves tend to venerate the Elven pantheon, though some still follow the 'old ways' of spirit worship. Both traditions are equally accepted, but the ways of the spirits is mostly lost, having been adopted and subsumed by the pantheon. Now, only the most remote villages and hamlets still exclusively follow the spirit ways.

The Elves have a small, but strong standing army. Being a forest people, they have little cavalry and instead rely on massed infantry to protect their formidable companies of archers. In times of great danger, the militias will be called up and it is expected that any able-bodied Elf will join up.

THE M'KOTT

The M'Kott

Physical Description:
M'Kott tend to be large, with the average male standing around 7 feet tall. Exceptional individuals may reach heights of 9 feet. Females average the same height as males, but rarely get taller than 8 feet.

M'Kott are enormously powerful. Even the average M'Kott is two or three times stronger than a well-muscled human. Because of their size and muscle density, M'Kott tend to be around 300 pounds. In addition to their great size and strength, M'Kott are extremely tough and physically resilient.

On average, however, M'Kott are not particularly intelligent or dexterous. While an individual may be quite clever, most seem unable to look beyond their basic needs. They are also best at gross physical labor and lack the finesse to craft anything beyond rudimentary goods.

History:
Recent additions to the land of Lachryn, the M'Kott appeared in great numbers after the Scale War. They spread rapidly throughout Lachryn and were soon omnipresent in the lands of the humans. The Elves, however, refused to allow them to settle in their forests and have kept this prejudice for many generations.

Culture:
M'Kott live in a clan or tribal system, where individual glory and battle prowess take precedence. Only one in four M'Kott born are female, so there is a gross disparity in the population. Therefore, most male M'Kott, once they reach adulthood, leave their home village to pursue their fortunes as soldiers, mercenaries, or simply as physical laborers. Their goal is to return home with enough wealth and fame to attract a mate and produce a family of their own. Many males, however, never return. Their lives are typically brutal and short, leaving them dead on the battlefield or in the service of some lord.

Traditionally, M'Kott follow a system of ancestor worship, with some great individuals having attained a sort of 'demi-god' status, in that M'Kott will try to emulate them and include them in their devotions, much as they would a grandfather.

One unusual aspect of M'Kott culture is the 'warrior oath.' M'Kott will often swear one or multiple oaths that they believe will protect them in battle. Some are rather simple, such as never drinking wine, while others are more complex, such as killing anyone who steps on their shadow. The breaking of these oaths is a great dishonor and M'Kott must perform very specific rituals to 'cleanse' themselves and regain the power of their oath. This traditional is slowly dying out and only the most 'backward' of M'Kott practice it with fervor.

With the prevalence of M'Kott in human society, many have abandoned the traditional life and taken to human ways and following human gods. They are looked down upon by more traditional M'Kott, who consider themselves 'real' M'Kott.

Pin-up by Erica Parks
http://klork.deviantart.com/

Pin-up by Sam Wood

Pin-up by Randy Kintz
http://rantz.deviantart.com

Pin-up by rkpost
daydream-graphics.com/artists/post

Pin-up by Jason Metcalf
http://jasonmetcalf.deviantart.com/

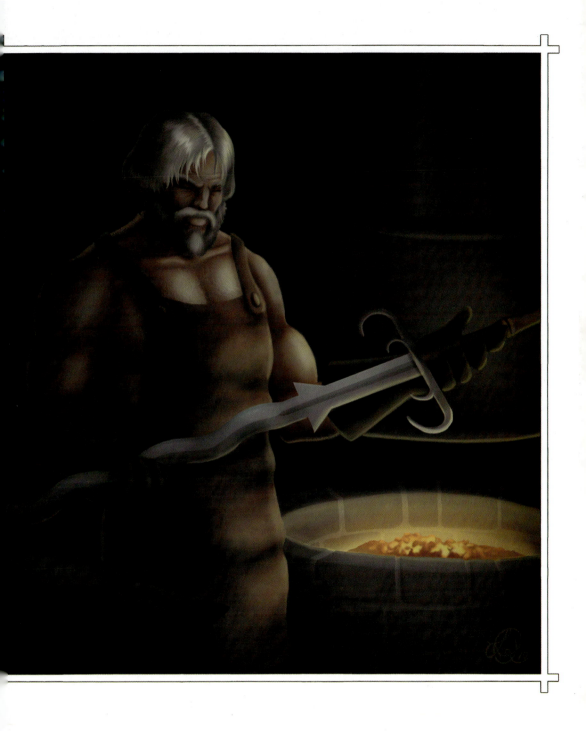

Pin-up by Leah Rivera
http://glenavon.deviantart.com

ABOUT THE WRITER

Born in Salinas, California, Jason Janicki was the youngest of four children. He grew up in the country and eventually attended Salinas High School and managed to not distinguish himself in any way, other than being good with computers, playing D&D, reading a lot, and not being able to get a date for the prom. He eventually attended CSU Fresno, majoring in English. During his time there, he learned to talk to girls, which lead him to meet Laura in fencing class and through her, Leigh Kellogg. Recognizing the intrinsic geekiness they both shared, Leigh and Jason hit it off immediately and began playing D&D together, in a game which is still going on today. Jason eventually graduated and worked for several years in Fresno, doing nothing of any importance. Leigh was eventually offered a job as an artist in Redmond, WA and Jason followed him up to become a video game tester. After testing for several years, Jason eventually became a game designer and has worked on a number of products. Wayfarer's Moon came out of a conversation several years ago, when Jason and Leigh joked about making a web-comic. Jason created a world and plotline and then completely forgot about it, until Leigh suggested they try to make a serious go of it.

ABOUT THE ARTIST

Born many years ago in Fresno CA, Leigh Kellogg spent much of his childhood sitting on his butt in front of the TV drawing superheroes and other things with capes. After high school (C.L.McLane H.S.) Leigh went on the CSU Fresno, where he majored in Art and Anthropology. In a college fencing class, he met his future wife Laura, and through her, Jason Janicki. The three became fast friends and began a D&D campaign that is still going on today. After graduating, Leigh thought about getting a doctorate in Anthropology but found that paying field work was rare and difficult to get. While trying to start a career in comics he found a job as an artist for a small, local computer game company. After several years of this, he was offered a much better position in Redmond, Washington and moved north. During this time, he worked on a number of computer games and eventually became an art director. Gradually this meant more and more management, and he found himself spending a lot of time in Excel rather than producing art. He suggested creating a web-comic to Jason, who surprised him with a ready plotline and characters.